Stinging of the Scorpion & Other Poems

Henry Victor

Stinging of the Scorpion

Henry Victor

Cyberwit.net
4/2 B, L.I.G.
Govindpur Colony,
Allahabad-211004 (U.P.)
India

Tel: 91-09415091004
E-mail: cyberwit@rediffmail.com
www.cyberwit.net

Stinging of the Scorpion & Other Poems
Henry Victor

ISBN 81-8253-062-8
First Edition: 2006
Rs. 135/-

Typeset by Vaishnavi Processors & Printers, Kamla Nagar, Allahabad
Printed in India at Astha Associates, D. N. Marg, Allahabad

DEDICATED TO

Chandra, my wife

&

Gitanjali, our darling daughter

CONTENTS

Stinging of the Scorpion

Last noon as I was enjoying my lunch
And engrossed in taste, below that table
Gently her tail bending, an ugly scorpion stung me!
Beast, then walked back a few steps and smiled
Even as I suffered with pain so excruciating
Friends across the table abundantly sympathized
With me now in stiff soreness, not daring
To bend and kill, or stamp with boot foot
The monster that hurt, earlier, my friend too!

Chaos to Creation

Strike, strike
Striking continuously
On the chaotic chaos on Sunday,
When there was none,
Truth was born on Monday
Practicing the same consciously
Led to justice on Tuesday
Playing fair, equally with all,
Peace arrived on Wednesday
Maintaining it
Ushered joy on Thursday
Rejoicing, all together,
Created beauty on Friday
When that which is pleasing was not exploited
Lovely creation evolved on Saturday

But 'self' ruled
And ruin re-entered on Sabbath

Strike, strike
On the chaotic chaos
Re-create truth…

Insanity

Yesterday
With might and main I labored
To diligently learn the art
Of lengthening simple shoes
For the ever expanding
Tiny feet of my little daughter

Today
I am frighteningly tormented
To discover the contemporary wisdom
Of conveniently cutting feet
To fit useless foot-wears
Made by the reigning professionals

Disagreeing
With the modern overnight professors,
I am very assertively informed,
By their cowardly counselors,
Is plain insanity
Fit enough only for dismissal

Ethnic cleansing
In the political arena is easy answer
For those wolfish rulers
Greedily striving to firmly establish
Corruptive power and stinking business
Instead, dealing positively, the prevailing pluralism

Busiest But Backward

Busiest
But the most backward
Place is my neighborhood,
Seen very little change,
While, I have passed
From childhood to adult life,
Being a boy,
Collecting leaves for goat
And firewood to burn,
To a university don
And a non-stipendiary priest

Life begins here at dawn
When children and men
Occasionally, also a woman or two
Visit the leftover shrub
To free themselves of the previous day's grub

This followed by the older folk
With un-fattened cows and slim goats
To graze the almost extinct grass
Then come those who catch fish
By stirring the stagnant pond
While the underfed stray dogs
Keep annoying the already frightened goats
Chained to their fixed posts

Towards the evening
But, only if there is no gun firing

The boys will be seen playing
Re-confirming, and re-confirming
The absence of my neighborhood's matriarchy

Later as the sun sets
The younger from among the older
And sometimes, even
The elder from the older
Trickle towards this busy camp
For cheaper but illicit strong drink
Patronized by the state's law enforcing machine

Busiest
But the most backward
Place ... !

Last Evening and This Afternoon

Last evening
With empty pocket
And two
Locally made grenades in hand
You fought, valiantly, those
That treated me as second-class citizen
Then I called you, affectionately,
"Younger brother"
And you, humbly, sat on my mat
Sharing my roasted meat

This afternoon
With your bullet-proof jacket
And pistol
With imported grenades tucked in waist
You order me to serve your interest
Treating me as slave in my own land
Calling yourself, arrogantly,
"Liberation movement"
Making me stand at your gate
Like a frightened rat

Iddiyappa Archi

Iddiyappam, the String Hopper
Symbol of life's complexity
With no beginning
Nor an easy end
Provided her a name
That the neighbours
Piously utter:
Iddiyappa Archi;
Her last name,
More of a title
Either for her age
Or, owning their linkage

Iddiyappa Archi
Knew not her, Sinhalese, parents
Ending as a servant
From the very beginning
Until Markandu, the Tamil, took
Her, in youth for his keep
When his wife
Couldn't provide him a child
Later he gently kicked her
When she made his wife's blunder
Providing her a thatched hut
That needed an annual roofing

Markandu, the wealthy
Cattle and land owner
Would venture to fix

His keep's roof, only
If he could remember her earlier body
And speak of his compassion
For another twelve months
But she knew to cope with her misery
With no cheating, no begging
Nor chasing, nor hounding
Wealthy gods and goddesses
Numerously present in the poor hamlet

Iddiyappa Archi, lights her bottle lamp
Disturbing not the rooster
Routine affected not even by heavy rain
Making string hopper
Muddalali to make his easy profit
Returning the remaining unsold
To feed her few fowls, only companions
Sharing her silent and spoken love
While providing a little luxury
Of not picking her fire wood
That she, now has enough
Even for final journey to *sudalai*

Note:

- *Iddiyappam* is a traditional Tamil and Sinhalese food, string (or noodles) like shape, from which, perhaps, the anglicized "string hoppers" was derived.
- *Archi* is a Sinhalese word for grandmother used also by the Tamil people to refer affectionately to the elderly women.
- *Muddalali* is the owner of a business concern.
- *Sudalai* is the Tamil word to the cemetery.

Soman Thambi

Soman Thambi
Harassed on Sunday
Arrested on Monday
Questioned on Tuesday
Tortured on Wednesday
Maimed on Thursday
Died on Friday
Buried on Saturday
That's the life
For Soman Thambi

My Mother's House

There is no water in my mother's well
And someone else, already, occupied her house as well
While she, to the new home, has forever gone
And my father too, will go there soon

My father retired at the age of forty-two
After serving the national army for years twenty-two
I decided not to return to my mother's place at forty-two
After living and enjoying it for years thirty-two

Into my mother's well, once I fell
To remember that, forever, very well
The house she lived was twice destroyed
Once by cyclone, and the next, by pogrom of genocide

About her house, my mother's thought, I shall never know
For sure, her well, quenched my thirst, and also more
While her house, provided space, for me to explore
And at the end, to my mother's place, I shall go

With Shoes on Feet!

A grab-and-run pack
A small survival sack
With one set of clothes for spouse and self
Passports, a file with just few mails
An old diary with addresses to contact
In England, Finland, and Switzerland
And some currency notes
Couple of thousands
In rupees that does not stretch
Like the American Dollars
They were what I needed most
As the pogrom was in progress
In my Tamil homeland
While I always went to bed
With shoes on my feet!

God's Tour

God decided to go on a tour to Lanka
Where the liberation struggles of the Tamils
Have emptied the tourist hotels
God did this tour via Montreal for reasons unknown!

God deciding to buy some Canadian products
To be taken as gifts for the people in Lanka
Went into Superstore hoping
To meet Anne at the till

God was yet to realize though s/he is omniscient
Even God's knowledge can be fallible
And things can go out of God's control
Despite s/he being omnipotent

God met Padma at the till instead of Anne
And became very furious
Screaming and shouting at Padma
God said the following:

"I provided you training in theology, and also in
Scriptures, both Hebrew and Greek
Not in mere translation but in their originals
Without neglecting liturgy and pastoral counseling

I had my own plans
When I taught you World Religions
Including Hinduism, Islam and Buddhism
Also the customs of Sikhs and Jainas

I chose you Padma for the services in Lanka
Because you are not only from that land
But also willing 'to bear the risks and pains'
In this hour of painful liberation from old and new colonial powers

I cannot understand how you could
In spite of the expensive training in theology
That you have received freely from me
Still waste your time on a till which you are not accustomed to

Not that one work is better than the other
Or one receives greater reward than the other
But the right person should do the right work
'What business has a dog in an iron bazaar?'"

Padma replied:
"O God! Be patient
It is not good to be impatient
For that is what our church leaders have always taught us

O God! I accept what you have said so far
But you who gave all these sound theological training
Did not give me the power to decide in your favor
Moreover, the Presidents and the Bishops
Are more powerful than you"

God was not convinced
But s/he was getting late
And that s/he might miss the plane to Lanka
After all what can Padma do
When Lankan Bishops do not want her there

God was just on time at the airport
And the touchdown at Katunayake was not much late

For that is the advantage of the Air Canada
At least that is how their own rate

The almighty slipped through the customs without any wait
But only to be received by a mighty bomb blast
The next God knew was that s/he was in bed
With plaster from the head to the foot

God was not sorry that this happened to the almighty
But s/he was surprised that neither the Bishop nor the Methodists
Cared to visit the Sovereign in the hour of God's need
But s/he never got angry with them

God almost had a heart attack
To see Anne at the Sovereign's bed side
But this time there was neither screaming nor shouting
For God did not want to embarrass the Bishop and the President
Who, were very loyally scratching Anne's fair back

Dog Menace

Hundreds of dogs,
Male and female'
Roaming the streets
In the land of singing fish

Dogs, regularly grabbing food
Habitually growling at the passer-by
Occasionally having a go on sex
But frequently fighting their own

More of other dogs as well
But with two legs less
Marching the very same streets
Demanding to be treated as gods

Reconstructing

With these bleak and busted building blocks
From derelict dreams of my exhausted mind
That my trampled soul has dared to dream despite
The bleeding wound in my badly battered body

This discarded child from that ruined family
That earlier neglected student of deserted village
Intends not to bend bruised knees to insolent might
Even if pushed into bankrupt economy of ghost town

With that broken pot and empty can the beaten spirit
Will continue on that abandoned boat to reconstruct
The wretched wrecked life and rebuild burnt house
Watering sun scorched plant in that parched land

Picking Cowry Shells

While wandering in eternity
I happen to be shipwrecked
And was surely stranded
In those isolated islands
Whose seas I sometimes
Easily crossed by swimming
While at other times struggled
Much to escape those pounding waves
Clutching currents, and swallowing whales
And when I did not have to battle
These monsters desperately desiring
To make short my looming living
I spent my silent moments
Picking up cowry shells
Whose smooth and glossy appearance
Attracted me, the lonely loner
Creating ceaselessly
A tranquil music in heart
And a sturdy hope in mind
That one day I will trade them
For a better life in a yonder world

Immigrant

Uprooting myself, and packing my belonging
Into just a small manageable size
But with a lot of hope, joy, and adolescent excitement
To encounter greater civilization, more humane humans
I am, now, an in-secured immigrant

Amusing, those few harmless in the host land,
Lamenting not their ignorance of other cultures,
In whose atlas is absent, the country of my origin; they
Excuse me, for the lack of their accent, and
Note of me, silently in heart: from distant planet, an alien

Instigate I, also anger and vengeance
Not in too many, but in few with evil and malice
To whom the whole truth - my economic welfare
Ruining their interests; and I,
Uninvited guest, to the land of plenty, imports
Diversity, that which they hate; to
Ease tension, they desire my leaving -
Room into which, for them, I am an intruder

Similar are not the other in greater number
To whom charity, but not informed by very plain
Reason for the commencement of migration,
And willingness to share their excess, the unwanted, with
Needy and poor, the wretched in sojourn,
Giving them a different identity; they gladly
Ease my burden, within their boundary
Realizing that I am, in midst of them, a powerless stranger

Gone back, I would have, to my own hell!
Unless there were those who speak truth in plain words:
Economic welfare of host-land, prime reason for opening doors;
Samaritans, they are, in the true sense!
To them, therefore, I am none but an honored guest

Uprooting myself, and packing my belonging
...
I am, now, an immigrant...

Spare Wheel

Sparsely used second-hand spare wheel am I
Tightly screwed down below the dark deck
Shut out of sight, sitting stoically nearer to street
I stroke, or touch not that passing path
Except in very, very rare circumstances
When one of them becomes indisposed.
But only for a dreadfully short moment
Then I am tightly fastened once again
In that very same stealthily secret space
In a planet where sharing is just a concept

Sparsely used second-hand spare wheel am I
Not inside an exciting sportive automobile
But in the precinct of wheeling and dealing of divine

Half Dead

I was on my way from the war-zone
To the peaceful territory when I fell among
Many robbers, who stripped me,
By paying a worthless small song
For my large land and huge property
They beat me with their traditions and prejudices
That made me appear a useless alien
And went off leaving me
Half dead while they multiplied
The easy profit of my hard toil
And my careful long term assets

Many priests did pass by
And took me with eagerness
To fill their pews and coffers
The Levites too followed them
Who stood by with their pious glance
To lift me to make me support their cause
Samaritans were too many
To hire me for cheap reward
Damning me in the permanent inn
Until I finished my green papers
To clean their stinking ass!

My Luggage

Fifty years of life, learning, and luggage
Five million rupees worth of asset
Ready to seek fertile soil, but at present
Reduced to seven pieces of baggage:

A Chinese alarm clock
A pan to cook Tamil breakfast
Coins to get to the airport
Carefully selected photographs

Dictionary to dictate denotation
Diary with names and addresses
Fabricius' Bible of 1777 (not for reading!)
Fennel seeds and Dianil tablets for excess sugar

Gifts for prospective friends
Games to play in the plane
Priceless papers defining degree
Precious documents permitting to 'pee'

Some cotton clothes for company and self
Sandalwood soap, silky socks and shoes
Underwear's to last only for some years
Umbrella to take cover from cosmic curse:

Arriving in the new home I discovered
Arrival of my luggage is to be delayed
While I rapidly learnt my sending root
Without withering too to be postponed

A Marriage Gone

Fortune great, she did not seek, but it
Is her intolerance of evil in the first
With which she could not co-exist, she deserted;
You, on the other hand, stretched your hand
For her to reach your apparent shinning hand;
An exciting experience you promised, with
Hour after hour joy and just peace
And soon the honey-moon was over;
Against her will, now, you rape erratically,
You, yourself with your lust for flesh,
For moments of petite excitement, and now
Ten times you have murdered her one self!

Wasps at Bee's Party!

A honeybee invited two wasps
Living in her neighbourhood
Entertaining the pair
With hard-earned sweetest honey
The wasps enjoyed the nectar
And hummed, and hummed
Among themselves
Leaving the bee to listen
To their rubbish buzz … zz zz …ing
Until the festive revelry
Adjourned for the day!

An Accent

To the pond behind my yard
I saw strolling a frog and a toad
They were there on that rainy day to breed
But the two soon began chatting their creed

Said the frog: "You a bastard *Bufonidae*
You disturb my peace with your croak"
Protested the toad: "You a rascal *Ranidae*
You scare me to my death with your squeak"

Friendly chatting now turned to a dispute
They leapt across belittling each other
And there crept the water snake, moving softly
Swallowed the frog, proceeding next to the toad!

Labelled Love!

Morning and evening
For five years
I tirelessly wandered
In that boulevard
Where read the billboard
"Love grown here
Watered by faith
Fertilized with hope"

But I roamed and roamed
And never saw love
Growing taller than sympathy
The weed
Flowering sturdy
And breeding speedy
In market I saw sympathy sold
In packet labelled - Love

Misappropriation

Misappropriating the language
Of love, I have seen many acting keen
The life of lust doing much damage
For themselves like that honey bee, drone

Temple cat too does not hesitate
To embezzle the sacred idiom
Much freely, more than a crafty priest
Thinking they are in heavenly room

Hypocrisy he hates more than denial
Intentions he inspects in the heart
Being true to ourselves is that full
What heaven above from us expect

Guantanamo

Desert winds howling through the mountains
Have ceased inside my ears that I am beginning to doubt
I hear the sea gulls crying for me who have no tears to shed
Slapping of the waves in "Guantanamo" is very painful
And my face is incurably swollen
The long hours of sedation has swallowed my sleep
And I wander, and wonder when I will sleep again
Permitting my mind to dream those mountains
My companions have been reduced
Those who admired my valour at one time
Too, seem to have departed
The new ones keep asking me the same question:
"Where is he?"
I know; I am in "Guantanamo"

Balcony

Pragmatism of that liberated mind
Declines detention to a deficient
Four by fourteen feet balcony
Shutdown at least for four months

Bare feet that knew every single
Sharp stone scattered in space
Of forty five thousand square feet
Want to walk with freedom

Balcony provides hardly legroom
With two wheelers willingly volunteering
For greedy North Americans piling
Garages with power over southerners

Two bicycles stranded in balcony
With no room to race, but relieving
The two plastic chairs salvaged
From earlier European garbage

Chained feet determined to hike
Clings to creative craft command
Surrendering not to tiny balcony
Sliding valleys and climbing hills

Stopping at Plamondon

When I'm sick in the city
I drive through the country
To see the farmland outside the city
But this time I did stop at Plamondon
To pay my homage to the Albertan men
Who canonized St. Isidore
The Holy Farmer from Spain
There I prayed for a celestial vision
And angels I did summon
To help me overcome the temptation
To enjoy the return
That I have never sown

Frost on Frosty Night

Whose woods these are, I'm sure, I know not
My house is not in any one of these hamlets
That I drive through this snowy evening
And my wife will not want me to stop here
To enjoy the Westlock woods fill up with snow

My Ford Focus will think it stupid
To stop when there was no skidding
On this icy road near the Devil's lake
With temperature below minus two zero
On the darkest evening of this year

The CD player sings it well
Expressing a pleasant mood
The only other sound is the engine
That warms my leg space too well
To keep me from freezing this winter

Roads are winding, slippery, and dark
Fear of deer, moose and coyotes
Keep me slow and hesitant though
But to my daughter I promised a hug
And kilometers to go before I sleep

Rich Beggar!

I'm poor, for sure a bigger beggar
But I too possess much, as peacock
Carrying a heavy tail, I my pride
That prevents me from easy begging

My neighbor, for sure, is very wealthy
Begging better than the big beggar
Carrying a begging bowl to pick mine
My praise, my pride, also my begging

But it is only that I walk with name
While the greater pauper walks with fame
Thriving on my poverty and that pride
That installs hell just here but too wide

By Waters of the Pacific

By waters of the Pacific I sat down and wept
Remembering the hundreds of immigrants
Cheated and let down by a culture of bigotry

On the weeping willows I hung up my violin
And my cymbals, refusing to sing
Songs of plenty and freedom

In the valleys of Rockies and spacious Prairies
My Caucasian hosts
Wanted me to sing songs of joy

But, how shall I sing the song of joy and freedom
In a land where the colour of your skin matters the most?

O Canada! If I forget my right, let my right hand wither
If I forget my honour, let my tongue cleave
To the roof of my mouth

O Canada! If I do not remember your filthy discrimination
Or, if I do not set my rights above my highest joy
Let me perish in this alien land!

Blessed is that one who takes up the cause
Of coloured immigrants and refugees
And does not dash their hope on rock of prejudice!

Mist and List!

Life I lived thus far is a mist, just a very long, long list
Lots of effects: I possessed and carried
On my shoulders and in my soul before I buried

Life I will live too is a mist, just a very long, long list
More effects: I wish to possess and I crave to carry
On shoulders and in my soul before I will bury

In the midst of this mist there will be a list
Of things I did and persons I will enlist
To agree with, or to protest against

But, at present, I know not my new list
Causes I may promote and concerns I must protest
In any case, at the end I take not a list
Nor will there be someone to take my list
In midst of another mist

Ascent, or Descent?

To label that as an ascent, or describe as a descent
I, with half a dozen degrees, still have not figured
That which I observed happening to Nicky,
My pet bitch, and to Jesus, the man from Nazareth!

When Nicky was full of life and in joy running rough
I saw the ticks finding Nick's body ticking with their taste
And when Nicky fell sick and laying nearer to her grave
I observed all these ticks, climbing down to seek more grace!

The same was true when masses saw Jesus of Nazareth
With words and acts shaking the Kingdoms of Earth
And when Princes of this World hunted the Nazarene
I observed all these humans deserting, leaving him alone!

To label that as an ascent, or describe as a descent
I, with half a dozen degrees, still have not figured
That which I observed happening to Nicky,
My pet bitch, and to Jesus, the man from Nazareth!

Bird in Bush!

Life I take in hand like grabbing the bird in bush
And begin to beat, bang, battle and bounce
As if I am beating, battling and bouncing clay
To make a flawless cup
From which I may sip, and at other times gulp
Deriving a pleasing taste for tongue
That my mind may announce to soul: 'indeed pleasure'
But only to end up with great pain
While my being fly and flee like the bird in bush!

This time I let life pick me like that bird in bush
Picking a worthless, wriggling worm
She picks, pecks, pinching me into pieces
To make me a faultless sup
For herself, her offspring, and then their poop
Deriving from my life a quick kick
While I mumble within my restless soul: 'painful pain'
A whispering not heard outside my heart
As life is perished inside the belly of a bird in bush!

Untitled

Your omniscience edges my conscience
And I discern you know my inside
Motives thoroughly; carefully you
Observe my travel and my resting

Your omnipresence wraps my presence
Fencing me very tightly where and when
I attempt to escape your attendance
No matter I'm in hell, or heaven

Your omnipotence makes me potent
Evolving mind and heart into being
In my mother's womb, counting bones I carry
Fathoming my all that is concealed

Fishing Within

I sit alone in my abandoned farmhouse
In front of this great, great silence
Far, far away from people
Busy doing this, that, and all those
That I do not do, and I do not have to do

In that quiet stillness
I thank you - you who have so well
Concealed yourself as that snow covered soil
But only making me, feel well
Your patent presence

I noiselessly thank you, the most mute
For those noisy, nameless, black-capped chickadees
Who, so faithfully, visit me and mine
And share my gifts of sunflower seed
Without ever prying into my privacy

I thank you for the frozen winter
That justifies my sitting
To fish within my self
That deep unclear pond, my own creation
Who's content, for me to conquer

This one life is inadequate
For that soundless surmount
Therefore you provide me
Another opportunity
In your eternity

And in the presence of your vastness of time and space
I loose all my anxiety to hurry up
To grab any garbage
That in any case I cannot
To your territories take

And therefore I'm grateful
To the boundless space that I enjoy
And I pray that you throw me into that
Unrestricted space of the distant star
And not into that icy world of the speckled trout

Memory and Forgetfulness

I'm amused and amazed by your solitary heart
From which, both my memory and forgetfulness
Flow into mine as your sacred gift, and a trust
That I need to employ in all my wakefulness

I'm baffled and bemused by those contrary elements
Operating within me, simultaneously, to embrace and reject
You, the prime source for my holding tight and that negate
Of your negating my negations of you and your rudiments

I'm certain and confident in your inclination for plural
Ways of dealing with that color and creed, both in multiple
That I will find special favor among yours, not unequal
Among the other, affirming that mine is never too little

Constant Treachery

When I go for copper
You give me a nickel
When I go for dollar
You give me none
Making me your slave
Bonded so permanently
To your constant deceit
And my colleague so treacherously
Announces: the divine mystery

The Lord is My Shepherd but I am in Want

The Lord is my shepherd; my needs are numerous
He leads me in the dry desert land
When I am thirsty
He guides me to rivers that are deep and flooding

He expects me to be courageous
Among those who are callous and inhuman
He presumes that I walk in the paths of the just humans

When I walk through roads that are dangerous and dark
I am terrified of the evil humans and their structures
Because though He had promised to be with me, I never see his face

Lord, you have very often let me down in the presence of my enemies
And you have forgotten to anoint my head with oil

My cup is empty
Yet, I will follow you
And serve your people always

You are My Shepherd

You have been my guide
Like a shepherd with his attendance
Pasturing his humble sheep
Making them to lie down on green pasture
And leading to waters still and clean

Your guiding presence I have seen
Every time I drive through Dunstable
In the darkest hour of the night

You pump into my heart courage
As I drive through pitch darkness
And I fear deer diving down my path

You inspire wisdom and fill me with patience
When my car have to wade through the knee-deep snow
While, in my mind, you keep increasing
A sense of alertness as I coerce
My wagon during total whiteout

You cover me with your blanket
When my journey is done
In temperatures below minus forty

You hold me straight
When I drive through
Roads that are winding and slippery

Surely goodness and mercy shall follow me
And I shall cherish your presence
That increases my resilience
Making me a good sheep
Walking to the butcher's blade to serve yours

Details

Details, details
When you have nothing
Worthwhile to talk
Talk of details

Length of his beard
Width of his garments
Seating arrangements
When he supped with his friends -
Circular, oblong
Rectangular, or something else -

Details, details
When you have nothing
Worthwhile to talk
Talk of details

The age of the ass
And the color of the colt

Experts on details!
You explore, and explode more details!
While the hungry are helplessly hanging
Around those feeding centers
And the penniless poor
For sake of development, suffer crucifixion

Talk of more and more details
Until the unseen evaporates,
Your face hidden behind masks,
While the anxious masses
Are disillusioned by your talks
And that Holy Week is utterly obscured

To Evelyn Menzies

Among your friends
I was the last to visit with you
My ignorance
The prime cause for my delay
But soon your contact
Made such an impact
And I'm here this daybreak
With your other friends
Not merely to conceal
In earth your feeble frame
But to canonize your lasting personality
While what you left behind in Barrhead Museum
Will surely bemuse many
Beauty
Was that you created much colorfully
Also artfully
With your flowers
In farm outside
And in room inside
Beauty
Was that you saw
In animals that crossed your way
And birds that flew to your window
Beauty
Was all that was in your soul
Beauty
Is all that you take
To your eternity
Simplicity

Was the costume you wore
Humility
Was the path you walked
Eternity
Is the destination you reached
Until I see you in that
Eternity
Good-bye Evelyn
May your soul rest in peace
And let light perpetual shine upon you

To My Eternity

Your whistling
I clearly heard
Your color
I see not
Your name
I know not
But
To my eternity
I take you

Peace

Brandon Richardson (1938-1985)

I envy your place, your peace
Your eyes that refuse
To see the vase broken
A brokenness braying into my being
Delaying my becoming
That stillness that you are:

Benches in Paradise

The hidden secrets this universe holds always fascinate my
Poor puny mind deprived of many prosperous opportunities, which many who
Sit in comfortable couches, (ceaselessly condemning carelessly, folks
On welfare of others - their left-over), are provided with;
The loss of prospects due to my poverty makes me shudder in
Front of tall thrones of judgment this world has set, with
Benches, wooden and hard, for people less fortunate;
In this planet of injustice and inequality,
Paradise is the only hope for victims of inhumanity

Red Lotus

Oh, the immaculate red lotus
The queen of flowers
The seat of Buddha
Tell me, this grown-up foetus
The secret of your excellent status
In spite of the trotting trend
That you grow in the muddiest pond,
In the stinking ground

Oh, the flawless red flora
The crown of vegetation
The seat of Buddha
How is that neither mud
Nor the filthy fluid
From which you derive your nourishment
Touch not your tender petals
Nor corrupt your fragrance?

To Breathe

Creative writing has become my breath
While relating to people
To find something common
Like that Good Samaritan
Sympathetic to man stuck on the road
From Jerusalem to Jericho

Hence I speak
To Amber, Ashley, Arsha
Brian, Brenda, Bethusha, Beeby, Benji
And other children screaming and shouting
While running to the Ice Cream Vendor

And I stop not so much to fix the jammed Ice Cream Car
Knowing too well of my ignorance of motor mechanics
But to feel the pain of man stuck on roads
And to admire his patience and persistence
To make the machine work
Though he carries not the tools
But only a heart for children
Belonging to rich and self-sufficient, shy folks
Considering themselves so important

Having seen this with eyes
And having felt this pain and pleasure
In pulsating heart I stop to record
Nay, to breathe!

My Envy

I envy the log
That disintegrates
Into that flame
That very death
And, and into ash
Reintegrating into her beginning
And, and final peace

I envy the raindrops
That deeply drowns
Into that ocean
That very death
And, and into vapor
Reintegrating into her beginning
And, and another creation

Chemistry Controls!

Unlike the orang-utan, my physical needs
To eat, drink, and have sex
Earlier I thought, was controlled
By my highly evolved metaphysical will
Being watched over by a guardian angel
Spying also my activities in that secret space

But after much struggle and constant defeat
I discover, very much to my relief
I cannot alter my chemistry that controls
And the present Master Chemist
Is that all-inclusive Merciful Ruler
Who leaves no space for another monster!

Short Life

Amazingly my heart joyously yields
Rather than struggling, fighting back
The unchangeable facts of short life:

Impermanence, as a bubbling bubble in the ocean
Soulless life with endless misery, ultimate essence

Languishing life that was not willing to ease
Openly I engaged to battle with hope of winning
Needs that were pressing towards permanent profits,
Gambling for an in-transitory large globe

Laboring always leading to the lingering languish
I began to sense the urgent need for change
For changing the repeated misery,
Easing the weight by accepting the facts of short life:

Impermanence, as a bubbling bubble in the ocean
Soulless life with endless misery, ultimate essence

Sourness against melancholy is now vanishing
Hour by hour, but not being replaced
Or transformed into an absence of wretchedness
Rather by a willing acceptance of the facts of life
Traumatizing every being that refused the transient nature

Wit and Wisdom

Life is too short, and time very swift, hence
Without wit and wisdom, just with strength alone
A path to accomplished success, and a closer
Friend, trustworthy to be trusted
Is impossible to be achieved, before
Death, which is deaf to our wailings, and
Without slightest concern for the age arrives
A steady mind, fixed firmly in the goal, only will
Witness, a witness to your death with work all done

Note: The poem above is an acrostic. The first words in each line read from top to the bottom will provide a proverbial challenge!

Millipede

Millipede bearing much empty numeral
Though with that stately maroon colour
You are empty within, like a barren shell
Curling cowardly, even for feathery finger

I see you as a symbol for those multitudes
In that body bearing name of the Nazarene
Single soul that withstood state power
Bolstered by a hypocritical priestly order

Best is Present!

Earlier when living with my own
Angrily I despised the out-worn
Saying: yonder was my dream world
That will fill purse and make me glad

Obviously, a mere word was not all what I uttered
Risking present, for better future, boldly I ventured

While in my dreamland
Easily I slipped into past
Secretly living not in a real world
That was calling me to adjust

Heeding not to the demands
Of the new present I kept talking
More of my earlier success
Even let going that was now in hands

I now realize, it is neither the past triumph, nor
Still to be born, but the real present that matter

By pulling my self together
Expelling all greed and delusion
Silently I learn to live the present,
To enjoy the moment that is current

Fashioned to Fashion

Your right hand formed me
While your left arm cuddled
My being towards your breast
And I'm now an earth-seed
I am flesh and blood
Aware of my scrawny self
Shaping, and re-shaping you
In my own indistinct, murky mind
Until I mature to bear
That fruit of self-giving
And my tissues are warm enough
To grasp and shield another life
The very purpose and destiny
That prompted you
To fashion, and re-fashion
My soul in your distinct image!

Jesus Lizard

Like Jesus lizard walking on water
I sail swiftly in my tiny boat
In this wide ocean, the vast world with dozen conflicts
Within that ever expanding endless cosmos
With me are two companions
Trusting my wisdom and strength!

I, in my voyage, pass the burial ground of dinosaurs
Colossal and robust creatures;
Those mortals of millions of years before
To live luxuriously dined on much morsel, leaving at end only a fossil
I stop here silently to meditate on my momentous mortality,
My pretensions of immortality welded well with my ego!

My team that I tug trusts totally
The speed I determine for my craft, a pace that's too cowardly
To recess to reflect under carpet, dirt and depth below
Lest vessel with squad sink into that deep ludicrous absurdity
Of half-truth, uninformed opinion, prejudice of every kind
Superficial love, charity not spiced with justice, and much more!

The Lord's Prayer in the Margin!

Our God in the margin
Help us cast away your marginality!

Let your rule move in from the margin
Let the distress of the marginalized
Be our prime concern
As it is yours in heaven!

Prevent us daily stealing food from the margin
Forgiving our ignorance of past plundering
Even as we begin, now, to release a little from the middle

Disturb us when we are complacent of the margin
Delivering us from our selfish affluence

For sovereignty belongs to those in the margin
For they dictate my faith, my practice
And even my seat in the hereafter
Now, and always. **Amen.**

Bedside Stool

Miles, and miles, I have carried
Carrying, on my shoulder, on my head
And also on my back
From bunker to bunker, I carried
Cherishing, protecting that memory
From every single aerial bombardment

Your bedside stool, a simple symbol
Painted in green, your choicest colour
Before I finally dropped
While over loaded with doubt
Of my continuing journey
Through that dreadful mire and dangerous sea

In any case, now I realize, in my journey
Beyond, in that ghostly world -
That you passed so long ago -
I must be very swift, and not delay
Where at the journeys end
I will find no room for a bedside stool!

My Unlit Grotto

I wait silently seated deep inside my unlit grotto
Listening to your footsteps falling rhythmically
Anticipate, my sum, but broken being knowing
Joyfulness emerging from the music of your hum
Negating desire for transient pleasure, trivial fun
Always willing to go through that purifying pain
This, now, has become my stable pre-occupation
I, your servant, therefore, endlessly entreat you
Governor,. and honored lodger of my unlit grotto

An Itch and a Twitch

My window curtains are wide open
I'm watching people on road ahead
Bound for some work, or returning home
With groceries and drinks for their kid

My mind too is not truly closed
I'm thinking thoughts of spotless gold
Bold and eternal, surviving coldness
Like that of Frost and Service of old

My spirit too is not in that rest
With many an itch and a lot of twitch
Like that damn deer dancing near the road
Finally killed by that stupid car

Flowers and Thorns

Let me neither linger
To gather flowers
To keep them
Nor to walk on
Anticipating for flowers
To bloom all my way
For what is important
Is to be on my way
To my eternal home
Through the path
That life has designed
Never grudging
But always appreciating
The flowers that bloom
And thorns that prick
For they are nothing
But providence, a grace
From heaven
For my incubation
And fruition

I Saw You Hanging

Jesus, I saw you hanging there alone
Like truth that needs neither props nor supports
Deserted by your studiously chosen apostles and
Disowned by Peter, James and his brother, the approved inner circle

Jesus, I saw you hanging on the cross
Like a slaughtered goat for public sale
Condemned by the elders who induced the masses to 'crucify'
Convicted by Annas and Caiphas the diligent chief priests!

Jesus, I saw you hanging at Golgotha, the place of sculls
Like a criminal with no legal practitioners to defend
Beaten with cruel hands, legs and whips
Belittled with filthy motions, petitions and abuses

Jesus, I saw you hanging outside the gate with your cassock missing
Like an un-ordained ordinary layman
Accused by both religious and secular powers that wish to stand apart
Avenged by Herod, the foxy culprit, and Pilate, the cautiously benevolent

Jesus, I saw the truth hanging there alone
With neither props nor supports to ease her suffering
Jesus, I saw truth hanging on the cross
Forsaken by both the elites and the masses
When truth didn't profit them

Jesus, I saw truth hanging at Golgotha,
The meeting place for sacred and secular
Abandoned by ministers of Church and State
While truth disturbed the status quo

Jesus, I saw truth hanging outside the gate
Humiliated and defeated, ready for burial
Because truth refused to compromise

Greatest Poet

The worlds around me are songs
You have sung thousands of years
The hills and the valleys, the sea and the river that flows
The smiling eyes of the younger and the older persons
And the wagging tails of the faithful dogs
The closet companion of numerous humans
In them I read nothing but the words of your poems

When I hear the skylarks singing
The wild and mighty elephants trumpeting
The frail human beings crying and laughing
While they struggle for their daily living
In them I hear nothing but the music of your harmonizing

O God then I turn to my writing that express my inner thoughts
Which my heart craves secretly to identify as poems
These songs of mine, I realize, are merely worthless words
That does not even produce rhythmic sounds
In them are lees and scum, which I desire to leave as trails

But yours is poetry with flesh and blood
That bestows life and love to entire world
To make my laborious heart and weary soul to leap and dance
And to sing unceasing praises to your unfailing glance
For you, and you alone, without any rivalry
Is the very source of both written and unwritten poetry
And in you I recognize the greatest of all great poets

Instill Within Me

Instill within me
An eager curiosity
Of the being
Which is thee
Grant me
An increase of
Bursting courage
To dive
Deeper,
And deeper
Into your being
Which has
No fencing hedge
Make my
Small self
Stone bold
To explore
Consciously
And consistently
The unexplored
Regions of your being
That makes me cold

Giving

We live
Not with
What we brought
But by
The generous giving
Of others

Even our being,
In short,
Is someone's giving

By giving we live
By withholding we perish

In any case,
What we have
And what we are
One day
We will be giving

Therefore,
It is better
That we give today
And give that
Voluntarily

Give,
And give now

Give
Not so much what we have
But give
Just our-selves

Give,
And give now
We
Like the trees and the cattle
Give
Not only
For the deserving
But also
For the undeserving;

Today,
We give
The smile they need
The time they require

We give
Not for ourselves
But for others;
Therefore,
We give
Not for recognition
And not for manipulation;
We give
Not for acknowledgement

We give
To those who ask
And
To those who ask not

We give
Because
We believe
In life

And
We live
Only by giving

Not Magic

Not a magic that I expect
You to quickly act upon
But a miracle that I yearn
In my life, you to execute

I do not ask you to change
My water into red wine
But transform my taste buds
That colorless will hint as wine

I do not ask you to multiply
My loaves, but that me
And mine never go hungry
Or ever disown the weary

I do not ask you for powers
To walk on the roaring sea
But that I will have the luxury
Of a friend, my woes to see

Not a magic that I expect
You to quickly act upon
But a miracle that I yearn
In my life, you to execute

To Happen

Nothing happens
Unless you make it happen
All have happened
For you to make it happen
Sit not, thinking that will happen
Or, someone will make it happen
For that will never happen
Until you make it happen
For it only happens
When you make it happen

Calm Me

When my restless soul
Is in fear and anxiety
Producing an unnecessary storm within
About the unfinished task
And the continuing work,
Calm those winds within my stupid being
Reminding the same to remember
Those mercies and moments of peace,
Considering carefully the many finished task
And the numerous yesterday's work
Which were all at one moment
Was in a state of fluidity
And with much uncertainty
Creating many stressful strain
Has, in fact, now been converted to joy

Unmask

Let my inner self
Dance and make merry
With energy newly released
That was earlier used
For masking of myself
In the land of men and women with masks

Let me neither resist nor curse
Those who persuasively, or even forcibly
Unmask the remaining masks
That I may at the end
Not miss the freedom and joy
Derived from walking without masks

Schooled

I was schooled
Not in the school
Of those scoundrels
Who, exactly know,
The way of success
And also, plenty;
This seemingly wise
Rebuked me,
With scolding
For my refusal
To follow
Their easy model

But rather
I was schooled
In the school
Of the trees
And those distant stars
While the clouds
Fair and dark,
Tutored me
To be free
Like the singing creatures
Of wings,
Large and small
To fly, and fly
Never to be afraid
Of want, height
Or, even failure

I was schooled
Until I learnt
The lessons,
To let go
While,
Those
Seemingly wise
Rebuked me,
With scolding
For my refusal
To follow
Their easy model;
Of success, and plenty

Folly

Folly is that which
fails to recognise your names
that others, joyfully give you
while I name you, the nameless

Deafness is that which
delights not, in praises to you sung by others
in Sanskrit, Pali and countless other languages
while I, in Greek and Latin, praise you, the ineffable

Blindness is that which
braves not, to discern your presence
in temples, mosques and shrines
while I, in Church, establish you, the boundless

Arrogance is that which
admits not the right of others
to follow, their chosen path
while you, always, remain the unfathomable

Forgive My Shirk

Grant me,
Oh the Nameless Name,
Unlimited forgiveness
And overwhelming grace
When I
In my nasty arrogance,
In foolish forgetfulness,
While breaking and smashing
Idols of clay,
Silver and gold
Tearing into pieces
Icons on printed-paper
Or painted canvas
Molded through extreme care
And drawn with patience so rare
Employing artistic mind
With untiring hand
Concurrently retaining
In the bosom of my petty being
The silly pride of my race,
Learning and other worthless achievement
In such way covetously
Ridiculing the tribe,
Tradition and other earnings
Of my numerous neighbors
Considering silently
My puny self more important
Than those who live
And toil around me
Entertaining and persisting
In that surest shirk,
The groundless superstition
That the sweetest sound
Is, surely, my own name

Synchronicity

A synchronicity in the number plates
I see of the automobiles
On the road in a given spot and moment
This increases my curiosity filling heart
With amazement
And my mind with a mull over
In all this, my number
Two three six remain at the bottom
With my will to synchronize the dissimilar
To create a colourful harmony
And recognize that underlying unity
Beyond the apparent dissimilarity!

Teach Me the Art of Tolerance

Open my mind O God
With unlimited love
That I may patiently
Consider the variety of percepts
Evolving from different human experiences

Increase in my heart
The desire to break away
From all small and partial rightness
While holding on to your truth
Which neither has boundaries nor fences

Teach me the art of tolerance
And beyond tolerance, the only way forward
Towards a new creation
For they are necessary not only
For our well being but also for our survival

Let me never resist or persecute
Not even discriminate against anyone
For what they consider to be real
Except when that sustains and breeds
Injustice and intolerance

Blacky, the Stray Dog

Blacky, the Stray Dog
Blacky, that's how my little daughter
Caringly christened Bruno, the stray dog
After months we also met his owner
That loved much, the four-legged creature

Blacky, at dawn would slip out of our yard
Even when we tied him with the strongest chord
After sun set he will need, never to be told
To keep guard of our unfenced fold

Blacky, had two homes to guard
With two titles, 'pet' and 'stray', together to hold
Daytime faithful to owner, chasing, always, any burglar
Nighttime compassion to stranger, driving, every evil intruder

Blacky, we needed so much in that garden
Closer to that lake, with no homes firmly planted
Pitched blackness was all, in night, that was seen
With tales of haunting genii that weren't benevolent

Winged Friends

Common house crow
Too much of a commoner
And often more of a nuisance
But without her the land
Will be infested with foul smell
An occasional darker raven
Lazy cuckoo laying eggs
For others to take care
The little cormorant company
Painting fence post near ponds
With their pee smelling of raw fish
Her elder cousin, the Indian darter
Alias the snake-bird
With slim and long neck
Scaring strangers screaming 'snake'
And the magnificent magpie
Whose number determines
Good and bad omen of those
Who falter and fail to value songs

These winged friends of my *oikos*
Tell me that black is beautiful
And much closer to nature's heart!

Black headed oriole with her beak
Pinkish, and her niece golden oriole,
The winged monks of saffron robes
To teach *dhamma* of easy flight!

Paddy bird, the widely spread heron
Of my *oikos,* standing tirelessly
In same place, whether in solid ground
Or stinking mud, an alertness
That makes fools call her blind heron
While her watchful eyes
Keep, in field, a close account
Of every extra toad that flirts

Ignorance prompts them
To call her *chavu-kuruvi,*
Death-bird, but she, the barn owl
Live for more, and more life
In nights guarding barns
From rodents of every kind
That attack seed paddy stored
For next season, a ritual gods
Expect eagerly from humans
In her sentry she is joined also
By her other cousins of varied
Size, colour and shape
The bay owl, wood owl
Fish owl, hawk owl, eagle owl
And the little jungle owlet
But all with their awesome eyes
And fearsome voice
Can announce death in life!

My Resume

An apple tree I never watered
But a wild wood apple
I tendered and cared for
As if I my self planted and watered!

A bred-fruit tree was my one time baby
I lost him, out of someone's negligence
A laxity I have already forgiven
And another one I shall not plant!

Coconuts, many did I sow
And have proudly harvested
Many more seedlings I did give
But I have not gone to pick the nuts!

Guava, many varieties I did plant
Fertilizing with much cow dung
Enjoying my little girl climbing
Like squirrel to leave half eaten for barbets!

Purple berry was the only big tree
That I bought with a young Palmyra
Both I let them grow wildly
For the crows to eat and perch!

Jack Fruit I did grow
Three in my mother's yard
And later, one in my own
But never did I pluck a fruit!

Papaw in row was my delight
Quickly they did breed
Making me look very wealthy
In that little hamlet I dwelt!

Avocado pear and pineapple
Never wanted to grow in my yard
Though much care I did provide
With enough water and also food!

Lemon and lime, they were in plentiful
With much ammonium sulphate
Detested by those earthly worms
Reminding me of my sin, polluting!

Plantain and mango I never had problem
With little care they did flourish
Like watermelon creepers and passion fruit vines
That I enjoyed pollinating flowers with brush!

Appa - My New Title

You bestowed on me
A title I cannot earn
Either by diligent learning
Or through much hard work
But it comes with much love
A warmer affection
Melting my heart
Exciting my whole being
"Appa", (dad) is that magic word
That finally brought poise
To a life of emptiness
Now, when you are not around
I go to sleep early
To hear that magic word
At least in my dream -
For I am at present a sure slave
To the comfort of that status!

Gitanjali

Gentle you were, in your smile
Involuntarily shaking limbs, until your
Tiny frame, into my hands, it slipped
Amusing me with gorgeous amusements
Negating in me those moments of meaninglessness
Joyfully, with tiny fingers
Affecting more life into my faltering being
Like the season of spring
Invigorating the shuddering mother earth

Vanished with your birth were
Ills that crippled us for fourteen years
Causing us to sing those songs
That makes God leap and dance!
Overwhelmed by a sudden birth, and
Remembering Tagore, we named you Gitanjali

Your Absence

I realize your brief absence
From home to visit with your friend
Makes me a frozen dead iceberg
And I shudder to imagine that one-day,
I must, with no excuse, let you go!

Your going away
Even for a brief moment
Makes that lively home
Into a funeral parlour,
An empty house
With dead, lifeless furniture,
Along with stuffed silent dog,
Dead, motionless picture,
The painted paper flag,
And the other unresponsive creature

All these, in full, come back to life
Only when you return with your commanding
Voice that gives meaning and cheer
Transforming the empty house
Into a lovely home, making
The stuffed dog to bark and wag her tail,
While the furniture wails and groans
As you hurt and throw down your weight
And the picture begins to move
When the flag leaps to life

I realize your brief absence
From home to visit with your friend
Makes me a frozen dead iceberg
And I shudder to imagine that one-day,
I must, with no excuse, let you go!

The Scarecrow

When you were hardly seven
You amused me with heaven
Your success in tricking Tina
With that hilarious scarecrow
That Tina mistook for a prowler
Into that garden of roses
Barking and barking
At the harmless
Steady scarecrow
With shoulders straight
And your torn frock for dress
And curd-pot for head
With face chalked on it
Your first artistic creation

Broken Pot

With a pot in my hand,
As a saffron clad monk on round
With a begging bowl in hand,
I am left alone to stand
Or walk anywhere to withstand
The hunger and thirst
The cold and heat
The cool breeze and the wind

With a pot in my hand
I am left alone to stand
To cook my food or to cover my head
To boost my height or add to my weight
To swell my might or uphold my right
To sell the pot, or at passers by to yell
I coolly could do any
For I am free of options too many

But one, I discovered
Which to me no one told
Yet it was they who revealed
With words they refuse to yield
Here, with wretchedness, I stand
With a broken pot in hand
Like a saffron clad monk on his round
With a begging bowl in hand

No Tears

Since all tears have been
Converted to thick ink
And I have been
Taught and trained by pen
None have I, to shed in vain

Furthermore, earlier, and even
Now, much of those tears have been
Expended for purifying my mind,
Heart and soul - no! My entire being
Teaching me the secrets of the unseen
And increasing my understanding of the seen

Those continuing tears eventually turn
To be the cement that holds my self
Together with those stray birds flying
With, already, broken wing,
The wretched of the earth

Noise and Ooze

My commode has been making noise
That my wife tried to fix it
Only to make it worse
And now it started leaking too!

By the time I saw it
The washroom was flooded
And I'm no plumber to fix it
Neither am I an idiot to avoid it!

So, I did with manly mettle, mettle with it
And tightened, at the end, the right nut
For both the noise, and the ooze to prevent!

We did leave home thereafter
I, carrying a washroom in ooze
While my wife, walking in perfect poise!